Soul Songs from Distant Shores

by Michelle Belanger

Emerald Tablet Designs ❖ Brunswick, Ohio

Soul-Songs from Distant Shores
Michelle Belanger © 2004

Cover photos: *Haserot Angel, Lakeview Cemetery*
by Michelle Belanger © 2003

Lay-out and design by Michelle Belanger

Published through Emerald Tablet Productions,
the publishing imprint of House Kheperu,
PO Box 1120, Brunswick, OH 44212

Photos by PendragonPhotography.com
And Michelle Belanger

For more information regarding this and other
works, consult the author's Webpage at:
www.michellebelanger.com

Contents

Illustrations

Introduction

The secret life of a writer is revealed through his or her poetry. Looking over this slim volume, which contains work spanning my fifteen-year career as a writer, there are certainly sides of me that are not evident in any of my fiction or prose. I ordinarily appear very detached emotionally, focused as I am on research and scholarship. But this is not to say I am passionless. Emotions, for me, come as brief, incandescent explosions, storms which toss me upon their tumultuous seas, and I can do little at the time but ride them out to completion. They are more intense for their rarity and their brevity.

At those times in my life when I have been overcome by a storm of emotion, poetry has been my outlet and my surcease. Poems have an immediacy to them, a depth of feeling that is difficult to capture in regular prose. As Wordsworth described in his famous preface to the *Lyrical Ballads*, poetry is a "spontaneous overflow of powerful feelings." Almost all of the poems collected in this volume represent just such a "spontaneous overflow." Sometimes the emotions I am writing out are terrible ones, but moments of passion, contentment, and insight have produced works just as profound.

Part of my purpose in publishing this volume is to share this other side of me with readers already familiar with my more scholarly demeanor. Over my years working with House Kheperu, I have developed this stoic, distant image as a result of my professional face. It was never my intention to make myself unapproachable, and I've selected the poems in this volume especially because they are very revealing of my human side. Many poems, like "Dance of Memory," were written in the heat of passion, while others, such as "Season of Madness," were written in a fit of despair. Nearly every emotion in between these two extremes is covered in these poems, from that "aha!" moment of

mystical insight to sheer exultation in experiencing a gift.

The poems here have already served their purpose for me. Each captured one of those incandescent moments of emotion so I can re-experience that moment of my life each time I read the poem. It is my hope that they will serve a similar purpose for you, inspiring flashes of emotion and recollection that allow you to recapture some past moment of your Self.

—Michelle Belanger

Transformation

Smoke and incense.
Luscious, curling.

A secret altar
in the space Between.

Your body and my body,
in rhythm, surging.

A fevered reflection:
flesh upon soul.

I am born and reborn,
in you, through you.

Clothed in fire. Shadow.
And the beating of great wings.

(1999)

The Watchers

It is the sign
of the more than human:

This strange dysphoria
with my form.

Possibilities
vibrate on the air
and in me.

Wings
somewhere
on the edge of being.

Ancient voices,
Names of the shining ones,
strange and symbolic.

The language
of the forgotten
whispers through me.

Something lost.
A great dignity
surrendered.

Sacrifice
or penance?

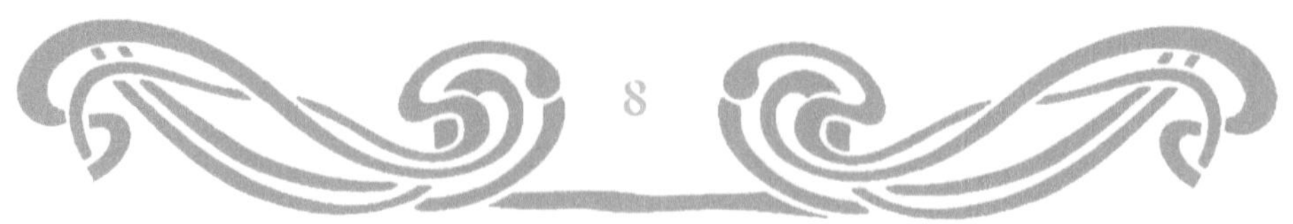

Our price for yearning.

The feel of mortal flesh:
the newness,
the trembling.

Yet the fires of Heaven smolder.
In my heart.
In my blood.

Are we fallen?

Not fallen.

We dared to see
the beauty of the forbidden.

We dared to hunger.
To desire.

We stood upon the edge of Heaven,
somewhere
in that forgotten time.

We gathered wings
about our golden bodies

and leapt away ---

(2001)

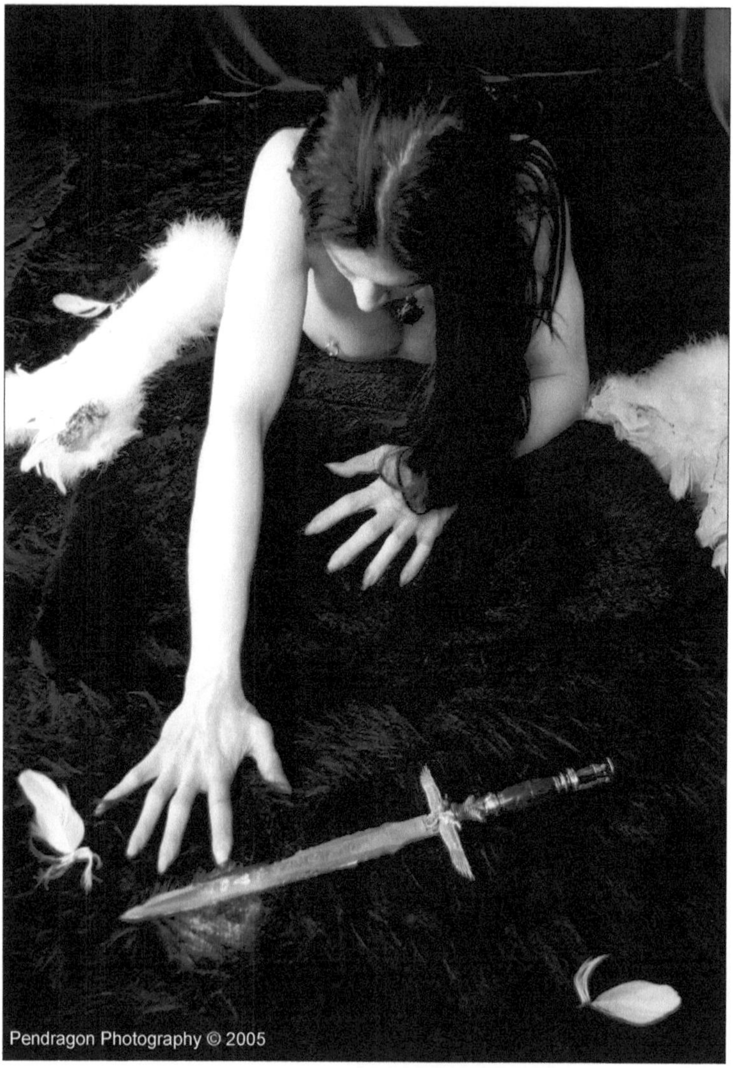
Pendragon Photography © 2005

Distant Shore

We fall into one another
like falling into sleep.

The night around us narrows
to the press of our two bodies
and that subtle, surging heat
which rises up beneath.

Hands flutter against flesh
restless butterflies alighting here,
now there,
each time pausing to drink.

I drink you.
Deeply.

We press forth into each other,
and the weight of you against my thighs
becomes all there is in the world.

You are music within me.
Convergence.
Rise and fall.
Two figures drifting
on an endless sea.

Wet and trembling we emerge,
new-born beings
clinging together
on a strange and distant shore.

(2003)

Pomegranate

This night —
sultry —
laps at the flesh
like a thousand wet, caressing tongues

The air is ripe as pomegranates,
pressing voluptuously
warm against skin.

It begs to be devoured,
sucked deep and long,
its innermost secrets pulled
from moist, delicate flesh.

Finally,
abandoned to the knowing grass,
rind and husk,
empty, upgiven,
quiver with the remembered touch
of relentless teeth,
ruby rivulets etched
upon alabaster chin
and those dripping
scarlet-stained lips.

(1997)

Alchemy of the Bedroom

In this dream-crossed twilight
Between waking and dying,
In this realm of thresholds
Where opposites meet and transcend into one,

Here in this bedroom sanctuary
Where man becomes woman
And woman becomes man,
In an endless alchemy of body and soul --

Here it is that we find ourselves
Having lost ourselves
Deep within one another's eyes.

There is no darkness
In the glimmer of candles,
Just as revelation illumines
All corners of our souls.

You plunge into me as I plunge into you
And with soul and body united,
We reach beyond both
To become a mystical whole.

(1997)

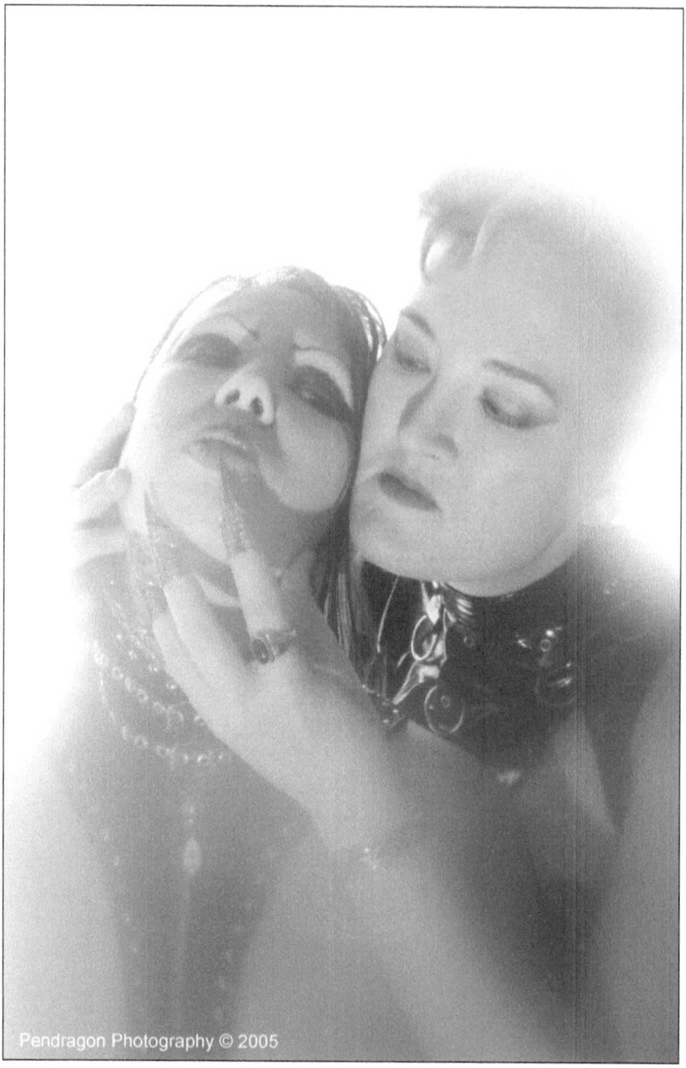
Pendragon Photography © 2005

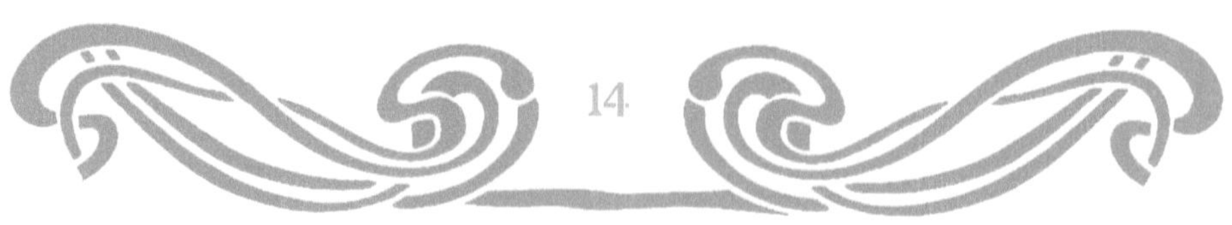

Consummation

You intoxicate me.
Your life is fire;
Each burning touch
Enflames me more.

I breathe you.
I breathe you in.

My hunger rages,
And the need within me
Is empty and cold.

What else,
But to drink deep your pleasure?
And in consummation,
You consume.

(1997)

Conundrum

I am a conundrum.

Man within woman,
Woman yet man,
I am Luna's heretic daughter.

My blood runs in cycles,
Yet I am Father, not Mother,
To at least one child.

What cruel trick has the universe played,
Giving me two roles
When there should be just one?

My body is hard and soft by turns.
My hips all curves, shoulders wide and strong --
To say nothing of what I carry between my thighs.

I am a walking confusion,
Not this nor that,
But the strangeness of all and none.

There is no solution to this puzzle,
For I am both lock and key
Fused together in one.

This works just fine for ancient gods,
But in this modern flesh,
What place do I have?

One or the other, they tell me.
Choose one, choose one.
Yet how can I ever make that choice?
There is no third door to accommodate
one such as me.

I have no pronoun for what I am,
No third box to check off on all the forms.
I am myself, whole and complete.

The deformity lies in all these half-
men and women, one part only
Borne in their flesh.

My flesh is alchemy, syzegy, pure —
The union of opposites
In chromosomal relief.

(2002)

Ozymandias Revisited

I met a wanderer from a darkling land
Whose haggard face and skeletal hand
And fathomless eyes, infinitely cold,
Whispered of stories best left untold.

He fixed his searing gaze on me,
And bore me down through memory.
I saw strange sights before my eyes,
With aged angels in antique skies.

There was a city between twin seas
Where despot priests ruled as they pleased.
They rained a fire across the land
With but a gesture from a thin, pale hand.

"All these things are yours," he said,
"For we are both the reborn dead."

(1989)

Union of Opposites

You burn beneath the alchemy of my touch,
Breathless, weeping –
And are transformed.

Flesh yields before relentless fingers and melts –
Sublimating into fire and water,
Blazing heat and trembling cold.

Fire and water fuse and merge,
Becoming something greater still.

The ecstasy transfigures your face,
Tugging cries from the depths of your throat
As if extracting the very elements of your soul.

I am athanor and crucible,
Destroying to transform.

You become the union of opposites –
Ecstasyagonypleasureandpain –
Till the last threshold is breached
And all becomes sublime.

(1999)

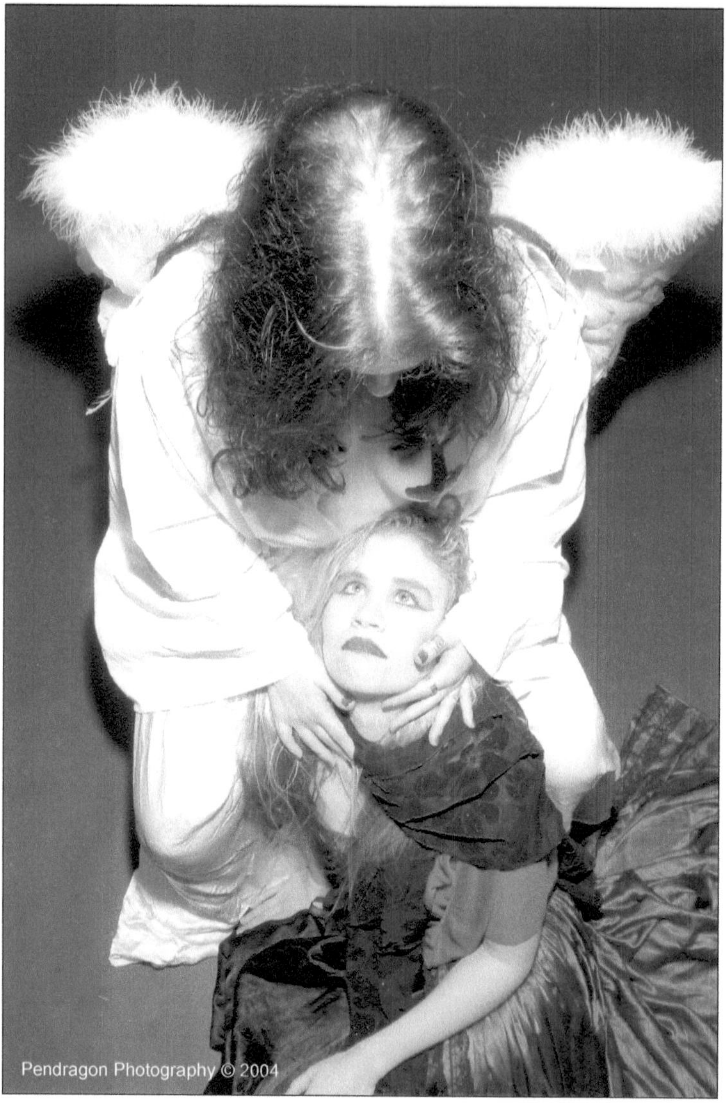
Pendragon Photography © 2004

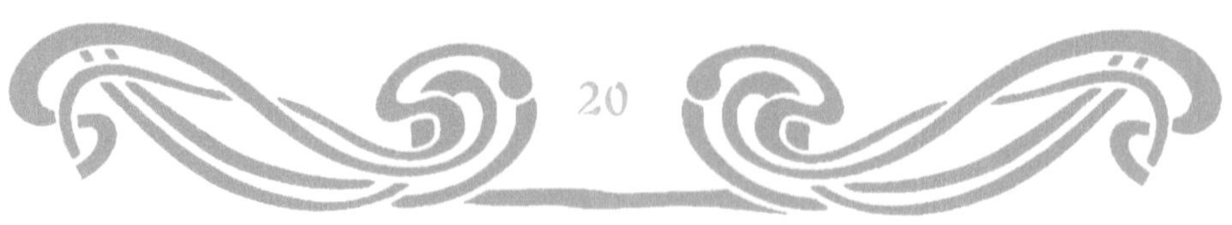

Dance of Memory

In the darkness of the curtained bedchamber
We awaken our flesh
As we awaken our souls,
Resurrecting half-remembered selves
With each kiss and caress.

The flesh is new, but the territory is old.
We have walked these roads before,
And the music and the dance of this lovemaking
Are the rote-lessons of our souls.

In the course of our exploration,
We strew the endearments and caresses
Of a thousands shared pasts
Across the space of this room.

The very air reverberates with agelessness.

And as the honey-thick incense smoke
Curls languidly throughout the room,
We taste its aroma faintly upon flesh,
Considering all those subtle things
That linger on the threshold of sensation,
Things that have no existence physical
Yet which our flesh can feel still.

(1997)

Invocation

Hush.
I can hear you in the silence,
Whispering invocations
And mouthing the Names.

In the space between spaces,
Your voice rises to me,
Each syllable a caress
That helps me recall my flesh.

With each breath, you recreate me.
Your hands move deftly,
Tracing the symbols and ancient signs.
I can feel them on me, in me –

There is darkness,
Then the shattering of light.
I am pulled across the threshold
Wrapped in flame and voice and word.

(1998)

The Twinned Soul

endlessly touching
but never touched,
forever reaching
but never seeming to grasp,
we who are so close
we cannot see one another,
we who are so entwined,
we reach out and hold hands
and think it is only our own that we grasp.

mourn for us, children,
and mourn for our lives:

we stare eye to wide open eye
and see so clearly
we think we are blind.
we are so much a part of the other,
we fear we are forever parted.
so together, we are forever alone.

(1990)

Awakening

To understand the song of the Universe,
you must *feel* it --

feel it with that part of you
that has lain like a fetus curled up in your soul,
silently, patiently sleeping.

Feel it with that ineffable vastness
which you have always known,
yet never could find a name for.

You will know it,
for there is a deepness inside you,
amazingly, achingly vast,
and yet hollow,

and when the reverberations of song
ring through you –

the echo of that music
will fill you at last.

(2003)

Voice

Poet (prophet)

consumed by words that burn
a sacred flame
holy (voice)vocation

voce
vocatus
speak in tongues

chant (rant)
call the God within
summon the spirit,
the slumbering flame

invoke it

vox, vocatus – voice

invocation

speak the Name.

(1996)

Excelsior

Be content? Fall dead!
Fulfillment is fatal.

Once satisfied,
What more is there?

When we no longer
Strive and yearn and hope,
Give us death.

What else is left?

(1989)

Harsh Muse

She lays
those burning lips
upon your brow,

and there is nothing to be seen

  except *her*

            vision,

which fades only after
you have tapped it out
in a frenzy
of aching knuckles

  and bleeding

            broken nails.

(2004)

(words)

words
are the links
in the chain
which imprisons
the mind.

the chain
wraps around
all the world
and enslaves
everything.

words
hold the key
to the chain
so be slave
or be free --

just beware
of the words
(all the words)
that you see

(1996)

Byron Remembers

Ada! Allegra! Augusta!
If only I could care …
But even now I am distant,
An outcast restless within myself,
So overwhelmed by my own passions
That I can barely turn my thoughts
To anything outside of *me*.

My lovers and my daughters.
The women who shaped and were shaped by me --
To say nothing of all my beloved boys
Kissed in shadows and abandoned come daylight.

Is there no justice? Is there no hope at all for me?
I am condemned to love in fleeting little bursts,
Reaching out with fervor
Only to touch and pull away.

I am a true vampyre, as Polidori said.
I devour all around me,
preying upon my beloved,
Yet never filling the emptiness within.

(2002)

Season of Madness

I.

I am writing my own undoing.

It is a tragedy in five parts.

The first part is blood.
That is where it begins
and where it ends.

The second part is love,
the Unobtainable.
Even when you hold it closest to your heart,
it is an illusion,
made crueler by your hope that it is not.

Love is a mythical figure in life,
a religion we have built our sanity upon,
hoping for redemption in a distant hereafter
which never comes.

The third part, it then follows, is unrequital,
while the fourth is disillusion.
Or dissolution.
Take your pick.

And it ends, again, in blood.
My blood,
blood-madness,
madness of the moon.

Hail to you Hecate,
you who revel in the spilling of blood --
Gorgo, Mormo,
Thousand-faced Moon --

II.

I have had my blood-letting
a hundred times.

Each time blood is shed,
it is different.
A new madness.
A new agony.

It is said that women are pacifists by nature
because as mothers who nurture,
and as wives who stand by the battlefields,
they are opposed to blood-shed.
Yet woman's very essence is in the shedding of blood.

Out of the ashes I rise with my red hair,
and I eat men like air --

Vagina Dentata.
She who gives birth in reverse.

It is subversive to reject the role of creatrix,
yet I would trade my occluded sex
for a vulgar phallus
any day.

And the Wheel turns round
through the seasons --

III.

Season of madness,
season of blood.

Moon-madness. Lunacy.
Hysteria --
It is just a woman's complaint,
after all.

Lock the madwoman up in the attic!
It worked for the Victorians.
There she can rant with the priestess of Delphi,
a gaping, bleeding Oracle
conceived in not conceiving.

Spirits! Unsex me here! --

I am too frail to be one
of the frail sex.
I have the heart of a man
and my heart is not in my madness.

IV.

Moon, moon, pale mother moon,
mother of secrets,
mother of Names,
key to the season of madness and blood --

Aye, this is madness,
but there is much method in't --

Silence me in my madness.
I rave. I ramble.
Yet there is inspiration in the well of madness.
Lunatics are the blessed children of
Pale Mother Moon.

Oracular, their great, round mouths
tilt up to her face,
filled to overflowing with moonbeams,
then bleeding forth pronouncements of fate.

V.

See what you want to see,
in you, in me.
You will do so anyway.
That is the nature of man.

Man makes the rules,
man defines the limits of reason, of madness,
then he interprets those rules
in the ways that suit him best.
Woman just bleeds.

It is easier to eliminate those
that question the rules
than it is to change them.

The rules define our world for us
so we don't have to think for ourselves.

Thinking brings pain.
Just ask me, the raving madwoman of these pages,
what agonizing labor it is
to bring forth thought
that has gestated days, months,
even years.

And never mind the breach births.
Zeus could tell you quite a tale
about his daughter Athene.

VI.

Knowledge is pain,
the pain of perception.
Perceiving the flaws,
the frustration,
the utter meaninglessness of the world.

This is the knowledge of pale Mother Moon.
This is the blood-knowledge:
the child you are destined to bring forth
is in turn destined only to die.
Birth is a sentence of death
without requital.

Woman thus does not create life
any more than she creates the potential
for more suffering and death.

O unhappy woman
who adds to the suffering
of this already long-suffering world --

pain-wracked Gaia,
agonized mother to us all.

What sorrow.
What agony to know it!
And the price of this knowledge is madness.
Madness and blood.

The blood-dimmed tide is loosed,
and everywhere
the ceremony of innocence
is drowned.

(1997)

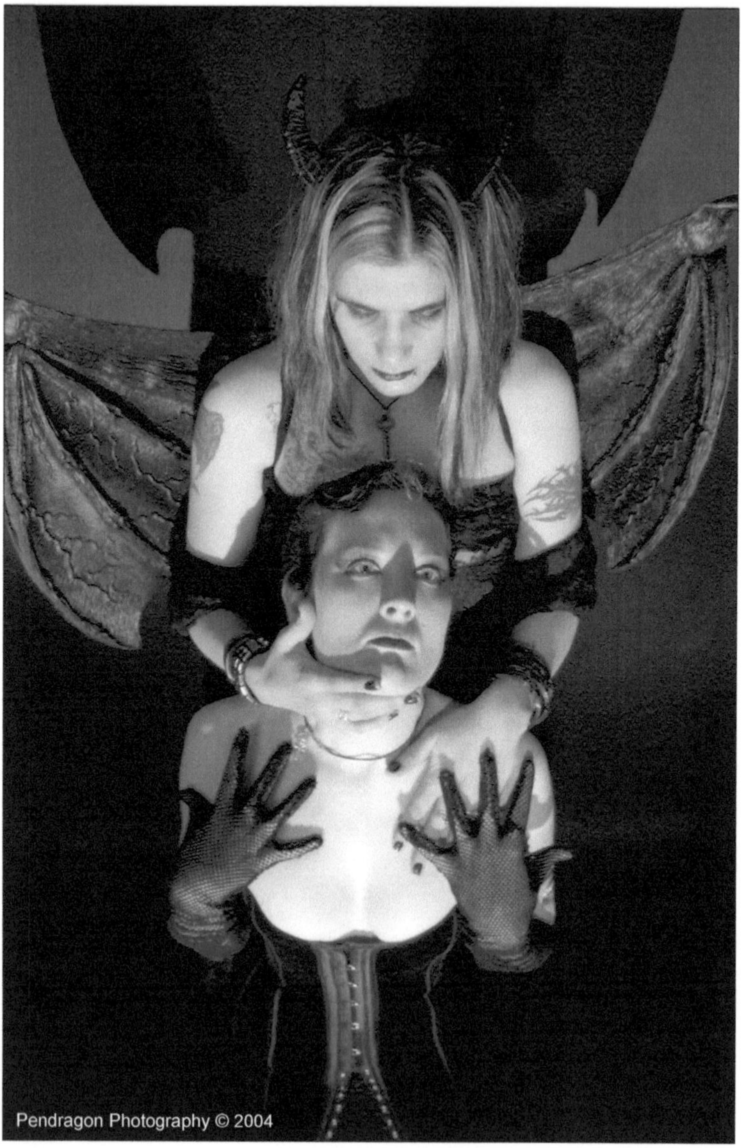
Pendragon Photography © 2004

Poems from the previously published

Darksong: Fantasies in Twilight

(under the penname Tasha L. Mourru)

Epitaph

I

Trapped in this vicissitude of dreaming,
I try to remember what life was like
and fail.

II

I am just shadow now,
intangibly clinging to a memory of flesh
I might have held
aeons ago.

III

I knew what it was like to love once,
but I've mislaid my heart.
I thought its ceaseless rhythm would lead me home
but the clock-spring wound down while I was away.
I hear only silence.

IV

Unspeakably empty now,
I wander this shadow-torn wasteland
searching for a memory of you.
I am alone.

V

The bones that strew this forgetting place
remind me of withered petals.
Brittle, many crumble at my touch.
Silently, I gather them.

VI

I fall to my knees
and gather fingerloads of dust.
Lighter than breath, it threatens to spin away
into emptiness
but I hold it together with tears.

VII

With bones my bricks and tears my mortar,
I erect a monument of you.
Vast, it strives against the colorless stretch of sky.
Starkly white, it screams of something yet inviolate
amid this endless wash of grey.
I remember what you were.

VIII

Engulfed by the huge thing that I have made of you,
I am no longer alone:
I am nothing.

IX

Dwarfed upon this endless plain of upgiving,
my task is finished and I am undone.
The last tattered shreds of self tear away
and I am lost
in the labyrinthine coils of your ear.

(1994)

Eurydice

Death is certain for the born.
Rebirth is certain for the dead.
You should not grieve for what is unavoidable.
-- the Bhagavad-Gita

wandering among the stones
lost within myself
i try to retrace those footsteps
that led me into this granite garden
far from you

voices tear through my consciousness,
weeping, beseeching,
calling my name
but i do not wish to answer
i do not wish to let go
there is music in the distance
a song as familiar as your caress

i find myself amid the goblin market
temptation upon temptation heaped up on plates
brilliant with the heavy glint of gold

i shall wait
i shall not betray my memory of you
those opulent hours we spent
in the splendor of the sun

i recall the story sung of mournful Kore
but one pomegranate seed
and i will be undone

seeking something lost
i find only myself
Eurydice huddled weeping
in the eldritch embrace
of silver birch
and whitethorn

have i ever known
any other arms
that held me with such strength,
such understanding?

there was something
but i've forgotten what
here where the light of the gravid moon
soothes stark granite and marble
into cool, pure silver
and flesh melts away
into brilliant, unburdened bones

naked
i spin atop an obelisk
reaching into the sky
and eating stars like candied dates

there was something
but i'm free of it now
the trees teach me
what it is like
to shed leaves endlessly
easily as the seasons command

there is nothing
but myself
and the understanding that a seed
must fall to the ground and be buried
before it can aspire
to oak

(1994)

Delusions of Flesh

(for David)

Tangled in the winding sheets,
you are the imprisoner of love-making.

Mute and sweating, you cannot even bear
to look upon your failed fumblings,
but carry out your blind search
enshrouded by the dark of night.

Fettered in the trappings of life, you are,
spread-eagled upon the bed
of your misguided passions.
Tortured and torturer, you cannot even dream
of the freedom of mortification,
but instead offer up sacrifices of tedious friction
to a deity whose eyes
are as blind as your own.

(1992)

Ianthe © 2005

Unmaking

> *But the natural reason is that [woman] is more carnal than a man, as is clear from her many carnal abominations.*
> *-- The Malleus Maleficarum*

It happens like this:
I sing songs you can't resist.
Repulsed and intrigued,
you long to flee
but only run further into the depths of me.

Vagina dentata,
I trap you like a fly,
impossible jaws closing
on the whole of you.
There is no escaping that which you desire.
I am truly Venus the devourer.

And in the dark of the moon,
I stumble through graveyards
gnawing on old bones.

Kali-ma, black lady,
lover and destroyer,
I give birth to infants in reverse,
feeding upon the new life you've given me.

I make men mine
by disemboweling them
then dancing on their corpses,
intestines twined about my head.
I am the one you love,
the womb that will unmake you.

Insatiable,
I eat everything.
No flesh nor bone
escapes my clasping lips.
My probing tongue knows
every intimate inch of you.

And when you fear me most,
that is when your desire flares hotter than ever
and you bow before me
in passionate supplication,
crying out for my other lips' caress,
and then screaming
when I bite you to pieces.

(1994)

Prometheus' Flame

(for Shelley)

You are my bedroom martyr,
your eyes alight with midnight fire
as I bend to worship
with supplicant kisses
the sacred temple of your flesh.

Pale Mother Moon
etches window panes
upon your bone-white skin,
arranging each curve and hollow of your face
into a snapshot landscape
of sharp light against shade.

Within your heart lies
Prometheus' flame,
its fires blazing forth
until you glow against my gaze.
My own pale flame
kindles coldly in my breast
and I long to reenact that fateful theft --

Driven by desperate appetite,
I rain libations of kisses down,
probing even deeper for that fabled well.

Ice encounters fire and melts,
blazing in a marriage of opposite poles.

With covetous fingers,
I grasp at your flame --
surrendering suddenly, there is no more
you or I or night or moon --

just *we*
in an explosion of celestial flame.

(1992)

About the Author

Best known for her occult works, such as the *Psychic Vampire Codex*, Michelle Belanger has been writing poetry since the early eighties. It was her passion for neo-Romantic poetry that helped inspire her publication of the Gothic literary magazine *Shadowdance* in the early nineties.

When *Shadowdance* folded in 1996, Michelle continued to dabble in poetry, although the bulk of her writing was by then devoted to the non-fiction works that have so firmly established her name within the Gothic, Pagan, and Vampyre communities.

Soul-Songs from Distant Shores is a collection of work spanning more than a decade. The bonus material from *Darksong* was previously published through *Shadowdance* magazine's imprint, Shadowfox Publications, and was released under the pen-name of Tasha L. Mourru in 1994.

For more information about Michelle, or to learn of her current and upcoming projects, go to her official website at www.michellebelanger.com.

FIN

www.ingramcontent.com/pod-product-compliance
Ingram Content Group UK Ltd.
Pitfield, Milton Keynes, MK11 3LW, UK
UKHW041836200726
13854UKWH00003BA/1174